T0365357

The
Baby Whale
And The
Surfer

Claudio B.

AuthorHouse™ UK
1663 Liberty Drive
Bloomington, IN 47403 USA
www.authorhouse.co.uk
UK TFN: 0800 0148641 (Toll Free inside the UK)
UK Local: 02036 956322 (+44 20 3695 6322 from outside the UK)

Because of the dynamic nature of the Internet, any web addresses or links contained in this book may have changed
since publication and may no longer be valid. The views expressed in this work are solely those of the author and do not
necessarily reflect the views of the publisher, and the publisher hereby disclaims any responsibility for them.

Any people depicted in stock imagery provided by Getty Images are models,
and such images are being used for illustrative purposes only.
Certain stock imagery © Getty Images.

This book is printed on acid-free paper.

ISBN: 978-1-5049-9941-0 (sc)
ISBN: 978-1-5049-9942-7 (e)

Print information available on the last page.

Published by AuthorHouse 07/09/2024

authorHOUSE

To Lorenza, Pier and Gabriel

The water colored blue curaçao was a distinctive feature of the bay of Playa Kanoa.

During the cold winters of Europe, whales passed by the islands with their young families. They were often accompanied by dolphins and many other types of fish

Whales, as you know, are great travelers and know all the seas of the world. But they particularly liked Curaçao, where the whale-tailed ones loved to hunt the shining fishes of Playa Kanoa.

Besides, this place was the only spot where children could play with the fast-coming waves that formed small ridges and crashed against the coral reefs below.

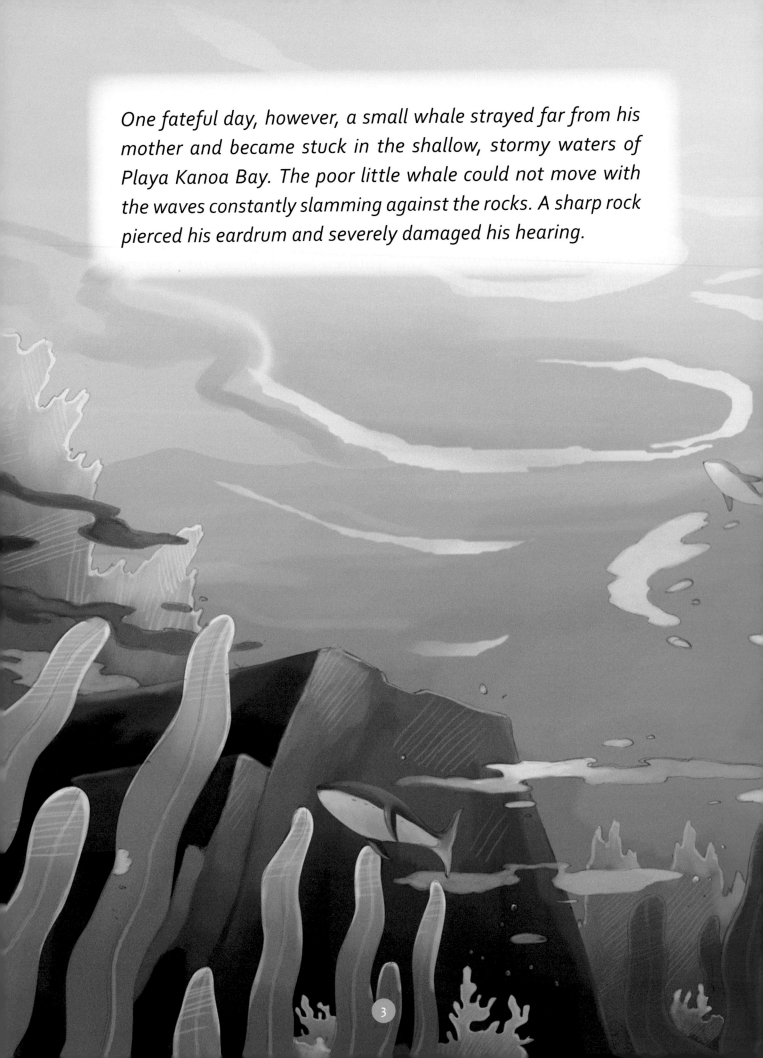

One fateful day, however, a small whale strayed far from his mother and became stuck in the shallow, stormy waters of Playa Kanoa Bay. The poor little whale could not move with the waves constantly slamming against the rocks. A sharp rock pierced his eardrum and severely damaged his hearing.

When the sea calmed the whale was shocked, but knew where he was. There was a problem, however... What had happened? Why did it seem that the sea no longer spoke to him? He could no longer hear the dolphins' songs or the sound of the waves—he was deaf! "Oh, maybe mom won't find me anymore"...he worried.

Meanwhile, Mother whale realized that her little one was not nearby and began calling for him, swimming back and forth along her route.

She passed Playa Kanoa and looked around, but the little whale was too far ashore and could not hear because of his hearing difficulty.

When the season of large waves began, surfers swimming from the shore discovered the whale, all alone and hungry. Since then, the whole community of the curaçao-colored sea, began to visit Playa Kanoa.

Soon, the whale stranded on the shore became big news and a discovery for all the island's children. Small boats moved in the shallow waters, bringing tourists closer to marvel at the wonder.

Far off the coast, in the vast expanse of the Pacific Ocean, the whale's family continued their journey, and Mother whale asked every sea creature she met if, by chance, they had seen her little boy.

One day, near the beautiful bay of Puerto Viejo in Peru, Mother whale saw a large group of surfers racing the waves alongside dolphins. She remembered how her little whale loved to play the same game.

The bay was very famous because, at the beginning of the world, the great sun god Pachacamac would contemplate the horizon and greet the dolphins, asking about happenings in other realms. There was something magical about the sea and the waves, perhaps that's why the dolphins kept returning to give birth to their newborns. It was a special day close to the shore where lots of kids were playing with their short boards. Fathers gently pushed their little boys to the peak of the waves, introducing them to a great passion. The strong current, typical when waves broke against the rocks, made surfing toward the center of the bay even more audacious.

Unnoticed, Miguel was gradually drifting farther and farther out to the open sea.

Suddenly, Miguel was so far out that his father began shouting, calling him back toward shallower waters. His father threw himself onto the longboard and started paddling, but at least one kilometer separated them, and little Miguel was too tired to swim against the elements.

With no more waves to catch and help him swim to safety,
Miguel became terrified of sharks lurking nearby.

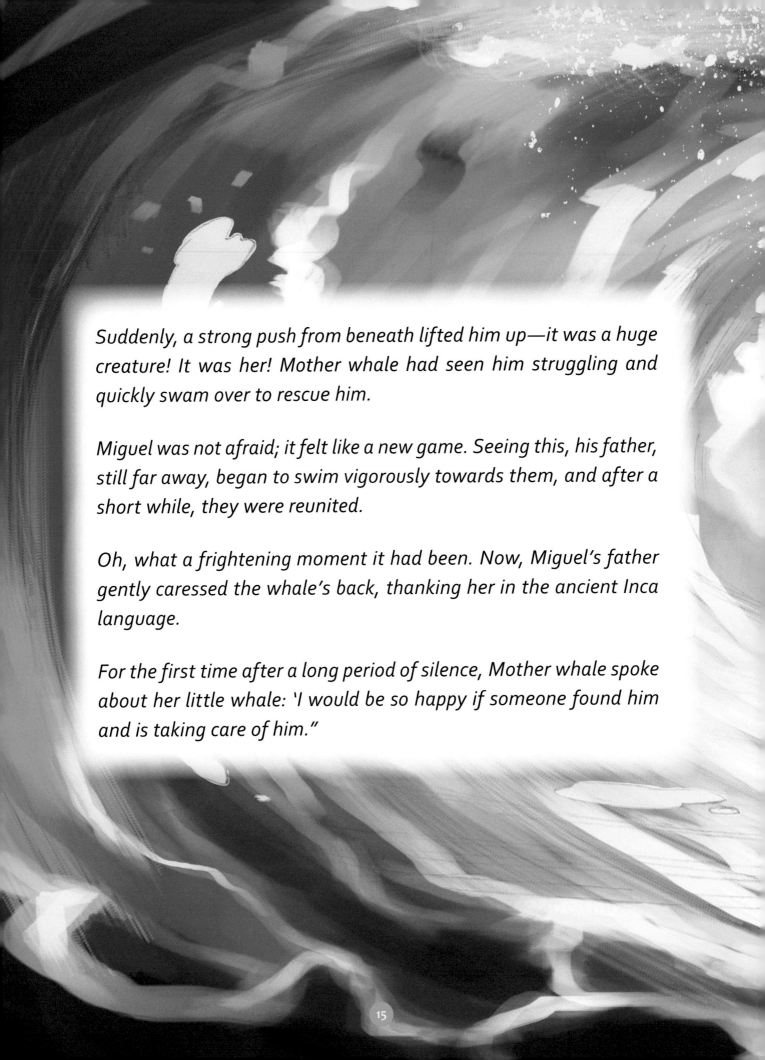

Suddenly, a strong push from beneath lifted him up—it was a huge creature! It was her! Mother whale had seen him struggling and quickly swam over to rescue him.

Miguel was not afraid; it felt like a new game. Seeing this, his father, still far away, began to swim vigorously towards them, and after a short while, they were reunited.

Oh, what a frightening moment it had been. Now, Miguel's father gently caressed the whale's back, thanking her in the ancient Inca language.

For the first time after a long period of silence, Mother whale spoke about her little whale: 'I would be so happy if someone found him and is taking care of him."

With tears in his eyes, Miguel said to his father, 'Dad, it sounds like the story your friends from Playa Kanoa told us." But... how could little Miguel know about Playa Kanoa? And what had his father's friends said about that distant place?

Filled with new hope, Mother whale resumed her long journey from the Pacific Ocean back to the Caribbean Sea.

The story of the whale had now traveled across all the seas. The residents of Playa Kanoa could no longer keep their treasure a secret. They called the experts from the Oceanographic Centre of Curaçao, who arrived by helicopter to bring the whale to the world's largest whale hospital, located in San Diego, the largest coastal city in California.

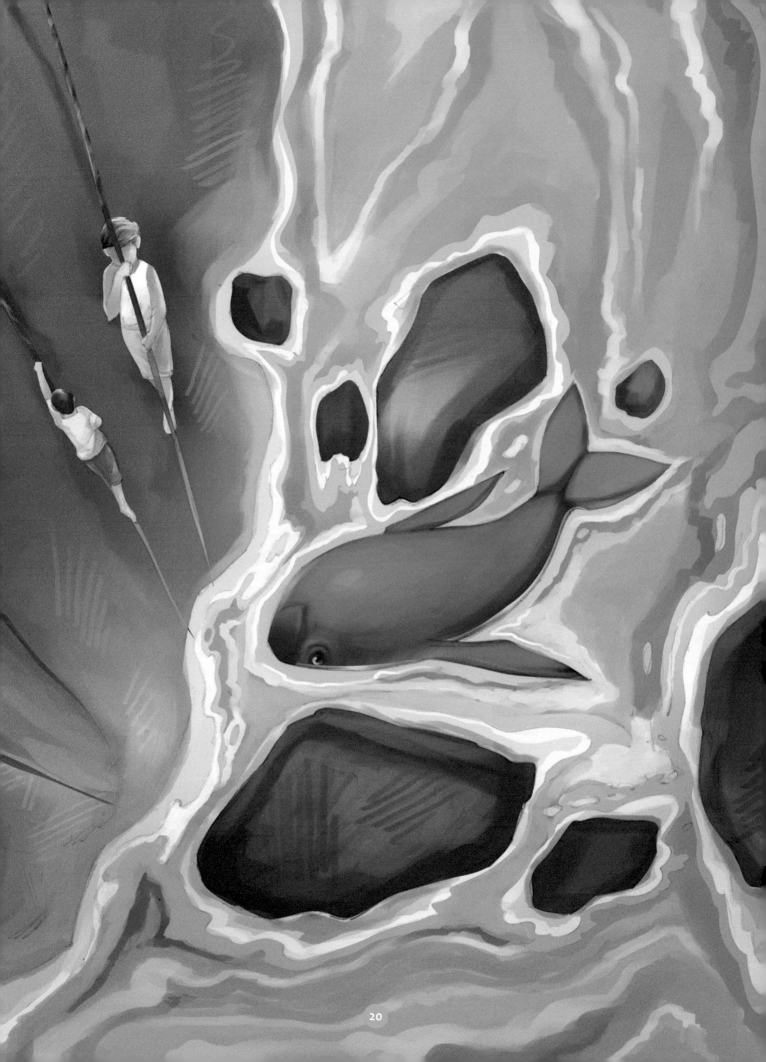

The whale began to feel the vibrations that spoke the language of whales, and when he was brought back from San Diego to Playa Kanoa for release, he managed to find his mother, who had arrived from the Pacific.

She embraced him with her large fin, and together they began to swim happily once again. "Mommy..." he said... "I never felt alone, but at night I was so said when nobody swam by my side".

Everyone from the small sea horse and clown fish to the big sharks and killer whales understood that there were men who loved their world and would always defend it from the disasters that humanity had caused over 2,000 years of history.

Printed in the United States
by Baker & Taylor Publisher Services